THE DINOSAUR THAT POOPED A PLANET!

Check out Danny and Dinosaur in their first adventure:
THE DINOSAUR THAT POOPED CHRISTMAS

To Danny & Harry, the most flatulent people we know - T.F. & D.P.

For Codie - G.P.

THE DINOSAUR THAT POOPED A PLANET
A RED FOX BOOK 978 1 782 95458 3

First published in Great Britain by Red Fox Books,
an imprint of Random House Publishers UK
A Random House Group Company
Red Fox edition published 2013
This book and CD edition published 2014

1 3 5 7 9 10 8 6 4 2

Text copyright © Tom Fletcher and Dougie Poynter, 2013
Illustrations copyright © Random House Children's Publishers UK, 2013
Illustrations by Garry Parsons
Copyright in this recording ℗Random House Children's Publishers UK, 2013
Audio recording produced by Patch McQuaid at ID Studio
Illustrated by Garry Parsons

RANDOM HOUSE CHILDREN'S PUBLISHERS UK
61–63 Uxbridge Road, London W5 5SA

www.**randomhousechildrens**.co.uk
www.**totallyrandombooks**.co.uk
www.**randomhouse**.co.uk

Addresses for companies within The Random House Group Limited
can be found at: www.**randomhouse**.co.uk/offices.htm
THE RANDOM HOUSE GROUP Limited Reg. No. 954009
A CIP catalogue record for this book is available from the British Library.

Printed in China

The Random House Group Limited supports the Forest Stewardship Council® (FSC®), the leading international
forest-certification organisation. Our books carrying the FSC label are printed on FSC®-certified paper. FSC is
the only forest-certification scheme supported by the leading environmental organisations, including Greenpeace.
Our paper procurement policy can be found at www.**randomhouse**.co.uk/environment.

MIX
Paper from
responsible sources
FSC® C104723

THE DINOSAUR THAT POOPED A PLANET!

Tom Fletcher and Dougie Poynter
Illustrated by Garry Parsons

RED FOX

Danny and Dinosaur liked to have fun.
Some days they had lots, some days they had none.

One day they were bored, they had no games to play.
Danny said, "Dinosaur, what shall we do today?
We could mow the lawn. We could tidy the place.
We could do our chores or we could go to space!"

"But you mustn't forget to have lunch," said their mummy.
"You cannot have fun without food for your tummy."
So they packed a packed lunch for the Science Museum,
Where rockets were kept if you wanted to see them.

There were hundreds of rockets and spaceship surprises,
Tall ones and small ones of all shapes and sizes.
And one that was ready to launch, with a door
Big enough for a boy and his pet dinosaur.

They ignored all the warnings – they couldn't care less.
They pressed all the things they shouldn't have pressed.

T-minus 5 4 3 2 1 IGNITION!
They started their intergalactic space mission.

They flew higher than houses,
and buildings, and cranes;
Much higher than birds,
even higher than planes.

"We're in space!" Danny yelled as they floated around.
But the dinosaur's tum made a rumbling sound.

"Is it time to have lunch?" Danny looked at his watch.
Then he looked all around for the dino's lunchbox.
Danny started to worry, then started to panic . . .
They'd left their packed lunches back home on their planet!

So with no food on board, not the smallest of crumbs,
A disastrous dinosaur feast had begun!

It gobbled up gadgets and gizmos galore –
    Nothing was safe from the space dinosaur.
Robots and ray guns and blinking red blinkers,
    Eating things thought up by NASA's great thinkers!
The hyperdrive-gamma-reactor-machine
    Was swallowed along with the space tractor beam.

It chewed and it chomped on the spaceship controls –
The rocket was dotted with dino tooth holes!
Inside it was bare, the spaceship was empty.
    Outside there were more things to eat – there was plenty!

It broke down the door
    with a cool ninja chop!
Out in space dinosaurs are
    much harder to stop.

It chomped on the moon like a big chunk of cheese,
    Then shoved even more in its mouth with a squeeze.

It munched on the Martians from Mars and their cats
  (Their cats are like ours, but their cats wear cool hats),
Satellites, Saturn and six supernovas,
  Shapeshifting saucers and seven space rovers.

It guzzled five gallons of fuel from the tank,
   And Danny's jaw dropped as he watched what it drank!
With a crunch and a crack and a nom-nom-nom-nom,
   In one dino gulp, their rocket was gone!

Now nothing was left — all Danny could see
Was a fat dinosaur where the rocket should be.
And so they were stranded with no way back home,
Just Danny and Dino in space all alone.

Now Danny was crying,

He cried
and he cried,

He cried and his
tears filled his
space suit inside.

Unless they were going
to stay there for ever,
The dinosaur needed
to do something clever!

With the feeling of guilt deep down in its gut,
Its brain brewed a plan involving its butt.
It knew there was only one thing it could do
To get them back home, it needed to . . . .

POO!

Like a poop-powered rocket the dinosaur flew.
    Dan hopped on its back and he watched as it pooed.
It pooped out the robots and ray guns and blinkers—
    The things NASA's thinkers thought up were now stinkers!
It pooped out the moon, it pooped out the stars,
    It pooped the space rovers and Martians from Mars.

When Danny looked back he could see a poop trail
From far out in space to the dinosaur's tail.
They headed for Earth and they started to orbit.
It pooped on the clouds,
but the clouds just absorbed it.

They flew past the buildings and streets of their town,
Leaving the houses all smelly and brown,
And finally landed back down on the ground.
"Hooray!" Danny cried. "We are home, safe and sound!"

They looked to the sky, and the things that were pooed
Had formed a poop planet right next to the moon.
And so Danny promised to listen to Mummy,
Because fun is not fun without food for your tummy.

. . . and just when you thought all the pooping was done,
a Mars cat plopped out of the dinosaur's bum.